'Twas the Night Before Santa and the Tooth Fairy Met

Gina & Mia Dowd

Illustrated by: Ada Litarowicz

For my husband, Brian, and my children, Mia, Joey & Maeve.
Love you with all of my heart.

Mom & Mike; love you lots, too.

Dad, miss you every day.

James is excited. It is Christmas Eve. He has a loose tooth that is ready to fall out. James is outside playing in the snow with his two sisters. They are bundled up but still so cold.

"If my tooth falls out and I put it under my pillow, the Tooth Fairy will visit tonight!" says James. "Do you think the Tooth Fairy will come even though it is Santa's night?"

"Well, I don't know if they know each other. Do you think they are friends? Santa lives in the North Pole but where does the Tooth Fairy live? No one really knows," stated Olivia.

"How can she live there? It's so cold and she always wears a dress. Do you think they have each other's phone number and email?" asks Daisy.

Everyone runs in the house and drops their jackets, gloves and hats on the floor. Mommy is baking Christmas Cookies. Lola, their dog, is very happy that the kids are back in the house. She is licking up the snow on their boots.

"Mommy, I have to make sure my tooth falls out tonight! It's a once in a lifetime chance to see if Santa and the Tooth Fairy will both come on Christmas Eve! says James. "A once in a lifetime chance!" exclaims Mommy. "Oh, my goodness. I've never heard of a kid putting their tooth under their pillow on Christmas Eve. I would imagine that they both could come on the same night."

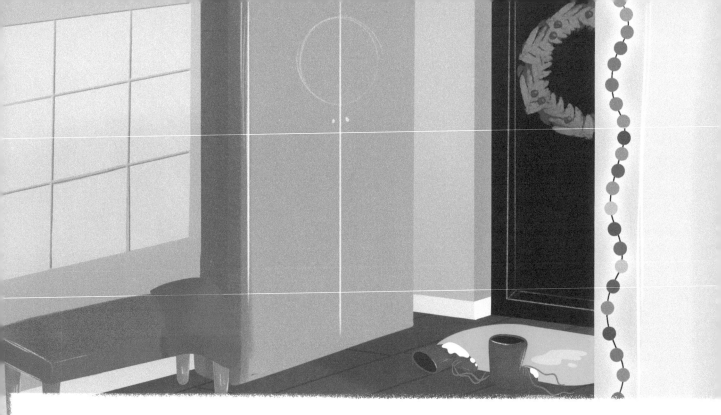

Daddy comes in the kitchen. He sees that Mommy is baking cookies and sneaks one off of the cooling rack. He slips one to Daisy.

"Thank you, Daddy," Daisy whispers with a wink.

James wiggles his tooth. It's getting looser!

"Do you want me to pull it out? I can tie a string to your tooth, tie the string to the front door, and slam the door! POP out goes your tooth!!!" teases Olivia. "No, that will hurt James!" says Daisy. "I haven't heard of them coming on the same night, either. These cookies are really good! James, do you want one?" asks Daddy.

Daddy hands a cookie to James. He gobbles it up. No luck. Maybe a gingerbread cookie would work? His sisters gather around James and watch him eat another cookie. He takes a big bite and out pops his tooth!!! The kids cheer and celebrate!

"Now that you guys ate all of the cookies and James' tooth is out, we still need to eat dinner and get ready for bed," says Daddy.

It's a snowy Christmas Eve night with plenty of stars in the sky to light the way fo
Santa and his reindeer. Santa lands on one side of the roof. He starts taking the gift
out of his sleigh. A fairy flies down and lands on the other side of the roof.

"Oh, Merry Christmas. I didn't expect to see anyone tonight," Santa announces. "Oh, hi. Kids teeth fall out every day. I know that it's Christmas, but I still have to work on holidays," the Tooth Fairy utters.

"Well, Christmas Eve is the one day of the year where I have to work the entire night. I actually have to get into this house. There are three kids that live here and I have to deliver lots of gifts," Santa remarks.

Santa and the Tooth Fairy are looking each other up and down. They are not happy that the other one has shown up tonight. Santa grabs his gifts and brings them over to the chimney.

"It shouldn't take me that long, I'll go first," the Tooth Fairy says with an attitude. "I have to go first. I have more stuff to do then you! Look at all of these bags that I have to bring in!" blurts Santa. "I need to get this tooth before midnight so scoot over!" says the Tooth Fairy. "Sorry, but this is my night to shine!" says Santa.

Santa and the Tooth Fairy both race to get to the chimney. They squeeze in and down they go! They land at the bottom of the fireplace in a tangled mess. Santa gets fairy dust in his nose and sneezes. The Tooth Fairy looks at Santa and is annoyed.

"Santa, you have to be quiet! I think James just woke up!" exclaims the Tooth Fairy. "Your fairy dust got in my nose. I never have fairy dust around me on Christmas Eve." says Santa.

Tooth Fairy rolls her eyes and pushes Santa's bags aside.

"You've brought so much stuff into this house! I just tripped and may have woken up one of the kids!" complains the Tooth Fairy.

"Well, excusez-moi but my "stuff" is pretty important," says Santa.

The Tooth Fairy crosses her arms., "This is not working for me. I usually work alone. I have to get James' tooth. But good luck with bringing all of your thingamabobs into this house," she says.

"I don't need luck. I've been doing this for THOUSANDS of years," Santa remarks.

Now, Santa and the Tooth Fairy have work to do. The Tooth Fairy flies up the stair
and into James' room. Lola sees the Tooth Fairy and starts wagging her tail. What
cute puppy! Lola gets so excited and starts to bark. She jumps up and tries to catc
the Tooth Fairy!

"Usually, dogs don't see me. What should we do? She won't stop barking," says th
Tooth Fairy to Santa.

"Hi girl!" says Santa as he bends down to pet the dog. "I speak dog so I'll quiet her down. I learned 478 years ago when I was in Timbuktu. Arf arf, woof, woof, bow wow."

Lola quiets down and walks to her bed. She lies down and falls asleep.

"Wow! I don't speak dog because they usually don't see me. Fantastic job, Santa!" exclaims the Tooth Fairy." We have to learn how to work together. You have a job and I have a job. The most important thing tonight is these kids," says the Tooth Fairy. "You needed me to quiet Lola down and I wanted to help," says Santa. "Yes, you are right," the Tooth Fairy smiles at Santa. "I'm sorry that I've been so grumpy towards you. We both have important things to do. Even though we are usually not here on the same night we can work together as a team!"

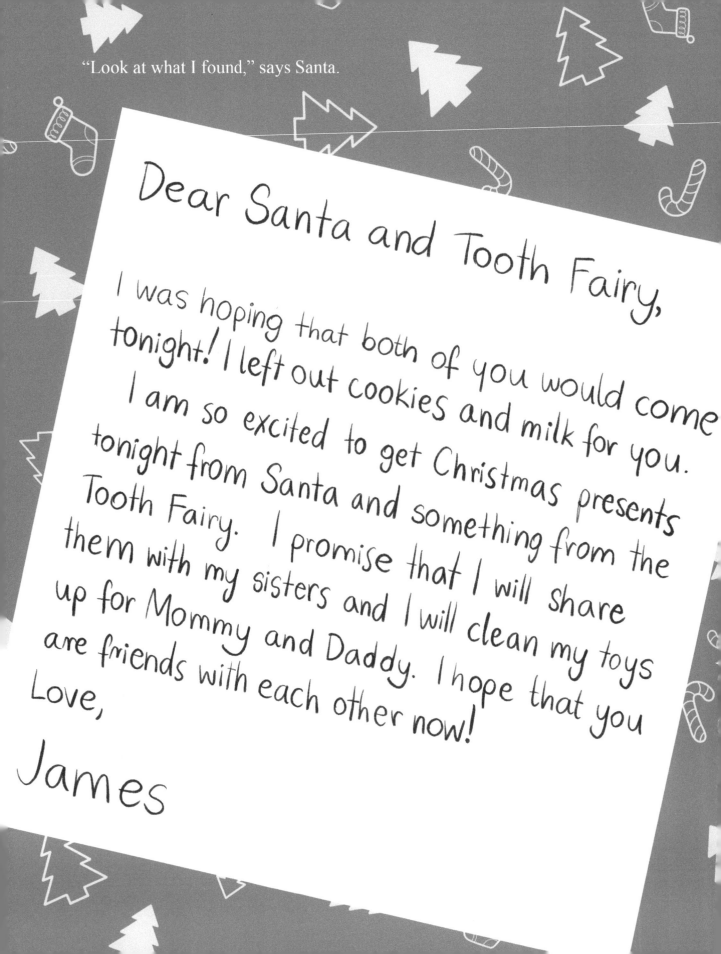

"Look at what I found," says Santa.

Dear Santa and Tooth Fairy,

I was hoping that both of you would come tonight! I left out cookies and milk for you. I am so excited to get Christmas presents tonight from Santa and something from the Tooth Fairy. I promise that I will share them with my sisters and I will clean my toys up for Mommy and Daddy. I hope that you are friends with each other now!

Love,

James

Santa and the Tooth Fairy smile and walk over to the table. "I think this a good reminder about how important Christmas and growing up is for these children. Why don't we do what James wants and let's sit down and have cookies and milk together," says Santa. "I think that is a wonderful idea," says the Tooth Fairy. "I'm glad that we got a chance to meet on this magical night. Maybe we'll see each other next year!"

The End

About The Author

Gina Dowd is a mom of 3 amazing kids. Former teacher and lover of books. This really happened to her 2 youngest kids on Christmas Eve and is what inspired her to write this book! Santa and the Tooth Fairy both showed up and left gifts, but no one knows if they saw each other that night. This is her first children's book.

Mia Dowd is in high school and is on the Lacrosse and Field Hockey teams. She plays Piano, Saxophone, Flute, and Guitar. She is in the Photography Club and loves taking pictures.

Find out more about Gina & Mia at
https://ginadowdbooks.pubsitepro.com/